A fabulous soaring thriller.

— *Take Over at Midnight,* Midwest Book
Review

Meticulously researched, hard-hitting, and
suspenseful.

— *Pure Heat,* Publishers Weekly, starred
review

Expert technical details abound, as do realistic
military missions with superb imagery that will
have readers feeling as if they are right there in
the midst and on the edges of their seats.

— *Light Up the Night,* RT Reviews, 4 1/2
stars

Buchman has catapulted his way to the top tier of
my favorite authors.

— Fresh Fiction

Nonstop action that will keep readers on the edge
of their seats.

— *Take Over at Midnight,* Library Journal

M L. Buchman's ability to keep the reader right in the middle of the action is amazing.

The only thing you'll ask yourself is, "When does the next one come out?"

The first...of (a) stellar, long-running (military) romantic suspense series.

I knew the books would be good, but I didn't realize how good.

Buchman mixes adrenalin-spiking battles and brusque military jargon with a sensitive approach.

13 times "Top Pick of the Month"

ISLAND CHRISTMAS

A MIRANDA CHASE ORIGIN STORY

M. L. BUCHMAN

Buchman Bookworks

Other works by M. L. Buchman: *(* - also in audio)*

Other works by M. L. Buchman:

Contemporary Romance (cont)

Love Abroad
Heart of the Cotswolds: England
Path of Love: Cinque Terre, Italy

Where Dreams
Where Dreams are Born
Where Dreams Reside
Where Dreams Are of Christmas*
Where Dreams Unfold
Where Dreams Are Written

Science Fiction / Fantasy

Deities Anonymous
Cookbook from Hell: Reheated
Saviors 101

Single Titles
The Nara Reaction
Monk's Maze
the Me and Elsie Chronicles

Non-Fiction

Strategies for Success
Managing Your Inner Artist/Writer
Estate Planning for Authors*
Character Voice
Narrate and Record Your Own
Audiobook*

Short Story Series by M. L. Buchman:

Romantic Suspense

Delta Force
Th Delta Force Shooters
The Delta Force Warriors

Firehawks
The Firehawks Lookouts
The Firehawks Hotshots
The Firebirds

The Night Stalkers
The Night Stalkers 5D Stories
The Night Stalkers 5E Stories
The Night Stalkers CSAR
The Night Stalkers Wedding Stories

US Coast Guard

White House Protection Force

Contemporary Romance

Eagle Cove

Henderson's Ranch*

Where Dreams

Action-Adventure Thrillers

Dead Chef

Miranda Chase Origin Stories

Science Fiction / Fantasy

Deities Anonymous

Other
The Future Night Stalkers
Single Titles

ABOUT THIS TITLE

Home for the holidays, with friends, should be worry free...

*For the first time in years, **Miranda** has invited guests to her San Juan Islands cabin for Christmas—her NTSB air-crash investigation team. She's not sure it was the best decision.*

When more of her past flies in on Christmas Eve, it proves to be an even greater challenge than she expected. But, with the help of her past and her team, perhaps she can find the feeling of that true Christmas spirit.

1

"Okay, I have a good story. On—"

"We've already heard that one, mate," Holly cut Jeremy off before he could even get out a second word.

Everyone started laughing, even Jeremy after he recovered from Holly's "friendly" wallop on the back. It had knocked most of the air out of him, and almost flattened him onto the wire racks of Christmas cookies waiting their turn.

Miranda didn't understand why all three of them were laughing.

She liked Jeremy's stories. Holly's were always so wild. Mike's often had strange plot twists she couldn't follow. Of the members on her NTSB air-crash investigation team, Jeremy's stories always worked the best for her.

If he was retelling a story, how could that single, two-letter word a sufficient clue for everyone except her?

Wait, this was one of *those* moments. The ones that she wrote down in her personal notebook for later study. She could picture the page heading: Appropriate

Reactions. Always a problem for people on the autism spectrum. But she was trying to get better at it.

When people laughed quickly, it meant...

A joke. She'd *missed* a joke. If they weren't amused by Jeremy's untold and as-yet-unidentified story, it was because... Oh! Cutting off Jeremy before the storytelling actually began *was* the joke.

By the time Miranda joined in the laugh, everyone else had stopped, leaving hers ringing alone in the cozy kitchen. She sighed, to herself. So, what else was new? She focused out the window on the storm clouds building to the west over Vancouver Island.

Mike nudged her with an elbow before he dipped the end of another coconut macaroon into dark chocolate and then a swish through the dish of sprinkles. "You got a joke, Miranda. Well done you."

He understood. He even said it softly so that the others didn't hear. Holly and Jeremy were busy threatening to face-paint each other with icing anyway.

She greatly appreciated that he never became frustrated with her about any of her shortcomings.

They'd been together as a team for a year, and Mike *always* understood. Of course, that was his job on the team: Human Factors—the one thing she understood least. Pilot error was a key factor of fully eighty percent of airplane incidents, yet remained a complete mystery to her. She could identify if it *was* human error or not, but the *why* was so elusive.

Undertraining, overconfidence, impairment, poor judgement: she understood none of those—except in herself. She'd striven her entire life to be better trained, remained possessed of a contrarian "confidence" that those efforts were wholly insufficient, knew her autism was a significant impairment in this area, which also gave her very poor judgment of people.

Mike's role was to ferret all those factors out on a crash.

She nodded her thanks to him for understanding her (also on her Appropriate Reactions page), and pulled the next sheet of gingerbread cookies out of the lower oven. She'd need three more sheets before she had all of the pieces to make this year's gingerbread sculpture.

Holly and Jeremy had apparently reached some sort of truce and were back to icing the cooled cookies spread on the maple-and-cherrywood counter rather than each other. Instead they had returned to mere verbal sparring. Mostly Holly sparring, and Jeremy trying to think of some kind of comeback. He was definitely the kid brother on the team, especially to Holly.

Was it natural for an older sister to constantly harass a younger brother? As an only child, she didn't know, but Holly certainly seemed to think so. Of course, she didn't pick on Mike much less, even though they'd been sleeping together for at least half a year. And that wasn't something Holly would do with a younger brother, so maybe it was just Holly. Perhaps she picked on everybody...except her.

"Why don't you ever pick on me?"

Holly blinked at her, then widened her eyes for some reason. Oh...surprise. "Do you want me to?"

Miranda thought about how often Jeremy ended up on the defense. "Um, no, that wouldn't be my choice."

"Well, there you go."

"But you pick on Jeremy and I would be surprised if that was his first choice."

"Righto, but our young padawan gets no say in the matter. You do." Holly wrapped her arm around Jeremy's neck, then scrubbed her knuckles across his scalp hard enough to make him squirm.

Mike just kept dipping macaroons.

Miranda decided she was better off focusing on her gingerbread.

Once Holly let Jeremy go, they returned to decorating the sugar cookies.

Miranda had provided them with piping bags of royal icing in several colors.

Jeremy was decorating snowflakes, Christmas trees, and Santas in neatly geometric patterns. She was quickly able to identify the crystalline structures on the snowflakes, and the branching symmetry typical of a Douglas fir tree. But it took her longer to identify the angle, force, and mobility-range diagrams of Santa's skeletal structure. She liked that, and wished she'd thought to do that in past years.

Holly's designs were messy enough that Miranda could barely recognize them. Her Santa cookies were all Mrs. Clauses, who appeared to be—Miranda looked away before she blushed too brightly—very undeniably naked.

Holly reminded her a little of Tante Daniels. She had always pushed at Miranda's limitations.

At first Miranda had thought that Tanya Daniels was merely a family friend who just happened to live in their house, acting as babysitter during her parents' frequent travels. After their deaths when Miranda was thirteen, she'd become *Tante* Daniels—German for auntie.

The day Miranda turned eighteen, their relationship was almost destroyed by the revelation that Tante Daniels was none of those things; she'd been a professional autism therapist, hired to help Miranda become as high-functioning as possible. It must have worked, because Miranda had found her way through the shock and anger to friendship.

And now, she had her team about her for a major holiday.

It was the first time in decades that there would be more than a quiet Christmas dinner for two, or just one as happened on the years Tante Daniels didn't make it to the island.

The cookies were Mike's idea. *Let's make cookie boxes for family and friends. Post-Christmas treats.*

However, who to send them to had become a problem.

Holly had been disowned by her family at sixteen, and her Australian Special Operations Forces team lay dead in some "Southeast Asian shithole."

Mike's one real friend had been a nun at his orphanage, who had long since passed away.

Miranda's two friends were Tante Daniels, and Terence, the head of the NTSB academy. He'd finally retired from field investigations completely. They'd both get boxes. That was two.

Which only left one for Jeremy's parents, and another for his married sister. Which made four.

Mike had said it would be nice to also make one big box for the Seattle NTSB office. She didn't know them very well as she had her own remote office, but Miranda liked doing nice things.

Holly, however...

Miranda eyed Holly's cookie decorations cautiously.

"Okay. Okay. No more naked Mrs. Clauses." Then she held up a pink piping bag, "How about some naked *Mister* Clauses? Think he's hung like a bull reindeer?"

Mike laughed, leaving only her and Jeremy to blush.

Miranda was a little relieved when Holly merely put the next cookie in a pink tutu and ballet slippers.

2

"IT'S MISERABLE OUT THERE," JEREMY WAS PEERING OUT the back door.

"You can stay inside. I'm used to doing this on my own."

But Jeremy continued pulling on winter woolen layers. "You've always lived alone here on the island?"

"No. My parents were here until they died. And then my therapist until I was fifteen and went to the University of Washington. I was only able to fly home on weekends but Tante Daniels was almost always with me. We even shared an apartment in Seattle."

"I meant since then. Since you were eighteen?"

"I lived off the island during my two masters degrees, and then whenever there were crash investigations that took me away."

"But you always come home here, alone."

"Except for visits by Tante Daniels, yes—until this team. It has always been my sanctuary."

"Some sanctuary!" Jeremy shove the solid-fir wood

back door open against the wind. She couldn't tell if he was being sincere or sarcastic...or something else. There was no way to check his face against her notes because he had a scarf over most of it.

It was one of those rare afternoons when the temperature in Washington State's San Juan Islands actually reached down to freezing. The snow wasn't sticking yet, but it had only just started. It would soon be shifting from cold kisses to sharp, icy poniards.

Twenty knots of wind made it colder. Jeremy was nearly tossed aside when another gust over thirty curled around the side of the house and slapped the door. Only the door's stout shock absorber, and his tight grip on the handle, saved him. According to the forecast, it wouldn't turn into a gale for several more hours. Not even a very big one then; winds at forty with gusts of fifty-five. At those windspeeds she could still walk, if she had to. Though gusts of fifty knots, sixty-three miles an hour, tended to knock her down because she didn't weight enough. Jeremy should be able to remain upright for ten knots higher.

At gusts of thirty knots, the winds only made her stagger about a bit—the closest she'd ever felt to what she imagined being drunk felt like.

Once the door was shut and latched behind them, she led the way to the garage. She stored her hay bales, made from mowing the grass runway, in the back. Opening one of the big bay doors, together they leveraged two rectangular bales into the Kubota tractor's front bucket.

As she was turning to climb aboard, Jeremy shouted

and stumbled into her back, nearly knocking her into the bucket.

"Hey!"

Jeremy just flapped a panicked hand toward the garage door.

Miranda looked over her shoulder, got the joke right away, and started laughing.

Except Jeremy wasn't, and once again she was on her own. She was fairly certain that was okay under the circumstances but wasn't sure how to be certain, so she stopped.

Cutting a string on the hay bale, she pulled off a fat flake, carried it out of the garage, and around to the side where the wind wouldn't simply scatter it aside.

The three deer in the doorway, who'd spooked Jeremy while staring longingly at the stacks of hay bales, followed her docilely outside. Jeremy brought up a distant rear.

"Up close, they're...big!" Jeremy whispered once the deer family had started eating the hay she'd spread out.

"Well, this is Rudolph," she rubbed the eight-point buck on the nose while he chewed a mouthful. "He is the biggest on the island, forty-two inches at the shoulder which is the upper end for sika deer. He's the island's alpha deer. This is Bambi. She's almost three now, and this is her second fawn. I'm thinking of calling her Thumper."

"Why?"

Miranda reached out to scratch the small fawn's rump just a few inches ahead of the tail. In response, she stretched out her neck and twisted her head

completely sideways, closed her eyes, and one of her
legs spasmed against the ground, making a happy
thumping sound.

"Oh."

Jeremy reached out to pet Bambi, who startled and
jumped away. Thumper raced to get behind her, and
Rudolph glowered at him. Jeremy stumbled back against
the side of the garage.

"I don't think he likes me."

"Bambi has always been a little skittish. Don't worry,
Rudolph rarely tries to ram people with his antlers.
Besides, we have to get moving, it's getting dark." Indeed,
between the heavy storm clouds and the late afternoon
hour, they *would* have to move quickly.

Once they were well away from the garage and the
three deer were returned to the small pile of hay, she
headed for the southernmost of the three feeders on the
island.

"I come here to Spieden Island so that I *can* be alone,"
she returned to the earlier conversation. "People are very
confusing, and *this* is my sanctuary."

"I like the sound of that," Jeremy stood on the rear
trailer bar and hung onto the roll bar close behind her.
"Though I'm not particularly good at being alone. Did
your family always own the island?"

"No. You know its big game history. We'd never do
that." Though she was less certain about her parents now
that she'd said it. They may have died when she was
thirteen, but she'd been thirty-six before she'd found out
they'd traveled so often and unpredictably because they
were CIA agents.

"Right, sorry. Craziest idea I ever heard. Turning a San Juan island into a hunting safari park."

Her parents had bought Spieden shortly after Miranda was born, but that was long after the park, set up on the island in the 1970s, had collapsed. Most of the larger wildlife had been removed, but she still worried about the Asian sika deer and Corsican Mouflon sheep during the big storms. They were so far from their homes in Japan and the Mediterranean. She'd considered trying to repatriate them, but then the island really would be lonely.

The animals already knew what to expect, and the deer and sheep were milling around the dark green hay feeder together. She dropped two-thirds of a bale into the steel rack, minus one thin flake to compensate for the third of the thick flake she'd given to Rudolph. Everyone pushed in to rip out a mouthful.

Then she saw the string between two of the feeder's top supports.

"Oh no!"

"What's wrong?" Jeremy squeaked as a Corsican ewe nudged him aside with its big curling horns; he'd been blocking her access to the hay.

"I forgot to give Rudolph any dried apple."

"What are you talking about?"

She pulled out the bag of dried apple rings she'd hung on the tractor through force of habit. "I always hang them on the string for the deer. They need it for the storm. We have to go back."

"What about this string? Don't these guys get any apples?"

Miranda stared at it. They did. But doing things out of order was so hard sometimes.

She took a deep breath.

"Tante Daniels always said that they needed it like comfort candy before a storm. I spend a week every fall picking up all of the ground-drop from the apple trees and drying them for the deer."

"Well, we'll save some for Rudolph. Let's do this one while we're here."

"Right. Okay. That's logical." She dumped the bag out on the seat, counted the rings, divided by three, then took four large slices from each third and set them aside.

After they'd strung up the third for this feeder, having to fight their way through the eager deer who wanted their share of the rings, she drove the mile and a half up to the far end of the island for another two-thirds—minus a flake of hay bale—and another third—minus four—of the apple rings.

At the final mid-island feeder close beside the small aircraft hangar, there were fewer deer waiting but more sheep. They placed the last bale and had hung the dried apple slices, when she turned and saw Rudolph escorting his family up from the house.

She was very relieved. Now she wouldn't have to worry about them during the storm. Considering their relative sizes, Miranda reallocated the twelve rings, five for Rudolph, four for Bambi, and three for little Thumper. The ratio of apple slices to body mass weren't perfect, but neither was she, so perhaps it was okay.

She'd started the tractor engine, as Jeremy was circling wide around the animals at the feeder. Very wide, as if he was still afraid of them. On the farthest side, he tipped his head. After a moment, he looked aloft.

Miranda killed the engine. Once it thudded to a stop, she listened as well. Up in the scudding clouds, an airplane was circling her airport. It was a private airport on a private island. So minor that it didn't even show up on the FAA Sectional Chart.

Only rarely did she have problems with people landing here. If they looked up this field specifically, they would see that landing was prohibited.

Yet the plane circled once more, popping briefly out of the clouds, though it was now too dark to see the profile. And the sound...was odd. It was a jet, but she couldn't identify it. Most jets needed more runway than she had on her island, so that could cause a major problem.

A crash to investigate on her own island was not the kind of Christmas Eve she'd been hoping for.

By the way Jeremy was tipping his head, he couldn't identify it either.

She yelped, spooking several of the deer, when the runway lights flashed on. They were on a radio-controlled frequency that only a very few people knew. And none of them flew jets.

Her radio was back at the house, so all she could do was wait and watch for the plane to circle down and make a neat landing on the runway.

The angle of the final flare and the skill at riding the island's notoriously squirrely winds to best advantage was the giveaway.

She squealed again, this time with delight.

Tante Daniels hadn't said she was coming for Christmas, but as the small jet eased to a halt close by the hangar, Miranda knew it had to be her.

And then she cursed to herself. She really should have recognized the Cirrus Vision SF50. It was the only production single-engine jet—just having the one Franklin engine accounted for the peculiar sound.

When she emerged from the jet's cabin, Miranda just raced up to her, and threw her arms around her.

"Welcome home."

Tante Daniels kissed her on top of the head as she always had. She was the one person in the world who was always safe. Even safer than Mike.

3

———

BECAUSE TANTE DANIELS' JET WAS SO SMALL, THERE WAS just enough room to tuck it out of the storm and into the island hangar. It was a close fit: on one side the Mooney prop plane that Mike flew the team around in, and on the other, partly under, her own taller 1958 F-86 Sabrejet fighter plane.

The Vision was very surprising. Sixty years newer in design, it was smaller than the Sabrejet by two meters, yet could carry seven people including the pilot in luxury, instead of one in a cramped cockpit. Of course, it couldn't break the speed of sound, or shoot its machine guns, or drop bombs as her Sabrejet once had, but it was a very pretty little machine with a very high-grade safety factor, including a built-in parachute system.

She would have liked more time to inspect it, but the storm was kicking harder with each passing minute. They locked the hangar door, then Tante Daniels and Jeremy clung to the tractor's rollbar as Miranda raced it back to the garage.

Safely inside the main house, they could finally speak without shouting over the wind's roar.

"You're still feeding the deer apple rings. That's so cute."

"You said it was important." Miranda hung up her coat by the back door and moved Holly's to another peg so that Tante Daniels could have her usual spot. By which time, Tante Daniels had hung her coat at the end where Jeremy's had been. He then hung his coat on Tante Daniels' peg. That wasn't how it was supposed to be.

The others didn't seem to care, so she let it be.

She'd followed them halfway to the kitchen but was still bothered by the order of the coats. Doubling back, she rearranged them because they might not care, but she did. If she ordered them all alphabetically, that left her own coat and Tante Tanya Daniels' on their traditional pegs. Then she organized everyone's boots to be directly under their coats, with hats and gloves lined up on the shelf above.

As always, by the time she entered the kitchen, Tante Daniels was on a first-name basis with everybody. Miranda had long since given up on studying how she did that, but she never failed.

As she entered the enveloping warmth of the kitchen, Mike handed her a steaming mug of mulled apple cider. It was her mother's mug, but Holly was already drinking out of her own mug, so she supposed it was okay.

She sipped at the hot liquid, enjoying the flavors and the way it warmed her insides. Everyone looked to be enjoying themselves. That boded well for them enjoying this visit to the island. She knew it was her job as hostess to make sure that they did, and so far everything was going well.

Mom had been a great hostess. Miranda remembered the big holiday parties that the Chases used to have here —people flying in from all over until every bunkbed in every room was filled to the limits. Other than the wake for her parents, which she'd spent mostly at the far end of the island sitting with the deer, this was the largest gathering since they'd died.

Holding her mother's mug made it all feel...okay. Mom to her. There *was* continuity here on the island.

And now with Tante Daniels, everyone seemed even happier to be here.

Miranda had always wanted to grow up to be her, even if she was several inches taller. Her platinum-blonde hair had transitioned effortlessly to pure platinum years before. Miranda's was still stubbornly brown; there wasn't anything else to call it but...brown. Tante Daniels' clothes were always effortless and sophisticated. Miranda had tried dressing that way herself, but site investigations and maintaining the island were far more about jeans and work shirts. In fancy clothes, she simply felt foolish.

Her boyfriend, Jon, kept asking if she'd dress up to go out on a date with him. But wearing something fancy always made her feel as if she was trying too hard and no longer was herself.

"Hold it, Tanya," Holly was smiling. "You told Miranda to feed dried apple rings to deer as a mental buffer against winter storms?"

Tante Daniels nodded.

"Aw! That's so sweet, boss." Holly squeezed Miranda's hand.

"I don't understand why. They need it."

There were some amused chuckles, but Tante Daniels did one of her waiting-patiently-until-Miranda-understood-the-lesson things. It made her feel as if she was twelve. It wasn't entirely comfortable.

The more she puzzled at it, the less she understood. "You said they needed it."

Tante Daniels shook her head. "I said *you* needed it. People were so difficult for you. So I invented the apple-ring dilemma for the deer so that you'd have connection to the animals and learn from that example."

Miranda dropped onto a stool, unsure of everything all over again.

"It worked, didn't it? As a little girl, you learned it feels good to help. It connected you to them. And now, you've connected to these people."

"Have I?" Miranda looked at her three team members.

"Hey!" Holly slapped a hand over her heart as if she'd just been stabbed there.

Mike was smiling.

Jeremy was unloading the two heavy grocery bags that Tante Daniels had moved from the plane into the tractor's front bucket for the trip back to the house.

The timer dinged for the next batch of cookies, and the others all were distracted until there was only her and Tante Daniels.

"I thought—" Miranda sighed, "—too much!" It was an admonition that Tante Daniels had said so many times to her as a child.

Tante Daniels nodded. "Remember to ask yourself how you *feel*. You hugged me on my arrival. You invited these people to your house for Christmas—which I think is both a surprising and a fantastic step. Were those logical decisions or are you connecting to your heart, Mirrie? It's a really good heart. If you doubt that, just go back out into that storm, and ask the deer. There's a reason they love you, and it's *not* only due to dried-apple rings."

Miranda thought about how she felt, and knew she was messing-up right away. Thinking about feeling wasn't logical. But she did *like* feeding the deer, always had. It made them so happy.

"I'm going to keep feeding the deer apple rings before storms."

"Good."

"Trusting you as much? How am I supposed to do that, Tante Daniels?"

She leaned in and kissed Miranda on the forehead. "That's good, too. Try calling me Tanya. Remember, I'm now your friend, not your surrogate parent or therapist. Maybe that will help me become a more real person in your mind."

Then Tante Dan—Tanya... Then *Tanya* picked up one of Holly's smiling, naked Mrs. Claus cookies, made it dance for a moment in a fashion that seemed surprisingly lurid for an iced sugar cookie, then bit off Mrs. Claus' head.

"Oh, that's a good sugar cookie. You haven't lost your touch, Mirrie."

"My gingerbread!" Miranda had forgotten about it

completely between her worries for the deer, and Tanya's arrival. "Tanya" sounded wrong in her head, but she would try it for a while, just in case it wasn't.

"All safe and sound," Mike pointed to the big cooling rack at the far end of the kitchen counter.

Miranda inspected each piece carefully. None were burnt, and they'd all cooled to a uniform crispness. Normally there were at least a few she had to remake, but Mike was as good as his word. They *were* all safe and sound.

"What are all these parts? It doesn't look like the house." Tan—*ya* came up to look at them with her.

Every year since she was a child, they had built a gingerbread house—this island home. The big, log-cabin-style lodge that had served as the resort center for the big game park, done in miniature.

"I'm trying something new this year."

Miranda wasn't quite sure why Tanya hugged her so hard, but as soon as she stopped, Miranda started working on the assembly of the gingerbread stand she'd designed to support the gingerbread sculpture.

4

THERE'D BEEN A LOT OF NOISE AND BANTER BEHIND HER, but they'd left her alone to work on her project. When she'd need a third hand to help her align a piece of gingerbread while she piped the royal icing joint, Jeremy was always right there.

Eventually he was helping her all the time. "Once I set the table, they really don't want me helping with dinner. I can barely make toast."

Holly was the master of the grill and claimed to be a top cook over a campfire but appeared as dumbfounded as Jeremy about what to do with a stove and oven.

Miranda just nodded.

She herself was a good cook, but not nearly in Tanya's or Mike's classification. Anyway, she couldn't think about helping until she had her gingerbread sculpture completed.

Jeremy started working on a side project when she didn't immediately need him, but she was too involved to look over. Only fifteen pieces for the base seemed like a cheat, but there were fifty-seven pieces in the main sculpture. By keeping the base so simple, that allowed her more time to focus on the main project.

Once they were done in the kitchen, and the smells of a cooking standing rib roast swam out of one oven and baking bread from another, Holly, Mike, and Tanya settled at the central dining table. There was talk, joking, and calls of "fifteen-two, fifteen-four, and a pair is six" which told her they were playing cribbage.

She liked the orderliness of cribbage, though she typically had to play the solitaire version as she was the only one on the island. It would be nice to go play with them, but she had to finish her gingerbread sculpture first.

Dinner was a definite distraction, but perhaps a well-timed one. It would be best if the first round of construction had time to set fully before she continued. She placed a light linen tea towel over it to keep it hidden from others...and from herself. If she couldn't see it, she was less likely to think about it.

5

"You never met such a determined little gal," Tanya told the others as she served out slices of her pumpkin-pecan Christmas pie.

"I think we might have run into her somewhere," Holly had her chair tipped back so far that Miranda had to look away before she fell.

"Do you know how many NTSB reports she read after her parents died?"

Miranda knew the answer to that one, "All of them. Just like Jeremy."

Tanya paused with a slice of pie on her pie server and looked at Jeremy. "You, too? All of them?"

"Yes, ma'am."

"Why?"

"Well, I was fooling around in Microsoft Flight Simulator, the professional version that the military uses. It's my dad's project. I had just crashed a C-5 Galaxy cargo jet. So, I wanted to see what I'd done wrong. That was when I ran into Miranda's second-ever investigation report, and I found out how *that* plane had gone down. Then I read all of the C-5's crashes. Most of them were before Miranda's time, but I liked her report best; it explained things so well. After that, I read all of the reports by Miranda Chase, and began re-creating each scenario in the simulator. If you ever go online and watch those videos that summarize crashes and have simulated footage for them, I did a lot of those early on. And once I got interested in plane crashes, I—"

"How did your parents not murder you?" Holly thumped her chair to the floor and took the pie that Tanya offered. Mike planted a large scoop of vanilla ice cream on the plate, then she set it in front of Miranda.

"Why would his parents murder him?" Miranda wondered if the pie and ice cream would murder *her* after so much roast and Yorkshire pudding and those peas with the little onions she liked so much.

"Self-preservation?" Holly picked up the next piece of pie from the plate, bit off the entire tip, then handed it to Mike. "This one must be yours, mate," she mumbled with her mouth full.

He served ice cream on it and set it in front of himself as if nothing was amiss.

Tanya was still assessing Jeremy with narrowed eyes.

"No," Miranda spoke up in his defense. "Jeremy isn't like me; I mean in any of the hard ways. He's not..." Tanya never let her say she was all *broken inside*. Unable to find the words, she just waved at her head. "He *is* simply exceptionally good at mechanical systems and computers." But he wasn't autistic. Didn't have to fight that cliff-steep learning curve.

Tanya was no longer watching Jeremy. Instead she was watching Miranda.

Unsure what to make of that, Miranda focused on eating her pie and ice cream.

6

THE HOUSE SLEPT. DESPITE THE HARD WINDS OF THE Christmas Eve storm, even the deer and sheep probably slept.

Not Miranda.

Instead, she sat in the kitchen at two in the morning, working on her gingerbread structure, and trying not to obsess about the prior evening—as if.

Jeremy was *not* on the spectrum. He never had to worry about who liked him or who was laughing at him.

He could tell that. He would know.

She couldn't and wouldn't.

Also, had Holly been teasing her about whether or not Miranda wanted to be teased, or was she not wanting to treat her like she treated a friend like Jeremy, or were she and Mike somehow using her as a metaphor for their own tumultuous relationship when... Miranda couldn't even keep all of the logical variations straight in her mind.

Finally, Tante Daniels—Tanya!—trying to change her

name after all these years. And saying what she'd said about the deer.

One of the things that Miranda's particular form of autism gifted her was a photographic memory for the words in a conversation. She—

Tanya sat down across the wood counter from her, her face shadowed by the darkness outside the range of her small worklight. Only a mug of milk clasped in her hands caught the light with a bright whiteness.

"When I was six, you said, 'The deer need an extra treat to get them through the storm.' When I asked you why, you said, 'They get scared. Dried apple rings will let them know it will be okay.' You didn't say *I* needed, you said *they* needed."

Tanya sighed. "It always surprises me that you can remember such things. Most neurotypicals, including me, can't. Even with my training, it's easy to forget that you can."

"Then why did you lie this evening?"

"The proper question is why did I lie thirty-some years ago. This evening I told the truth. You needed connection so badly. Your father was only interested in seeing what your *mind* was capable of achieving—what parent has their child working on cracking secret codes at eight that even the CIA can't unravel? Your mother was deeply overwhelmed by you and her own sense of incompetence and inferiority. Unjustified on both counts I might add; she loved you very much which fixes almost everything, and she was an exceptional woman who I still miss so much. It makes it very hard to come back here sometimes."

Miranda had never thought about what her parents' deaths must have been like for Tanya. When she reached a hand across the counter, Tanya clasped it hard before she continued.

"But that's why they hired me. I was fresh out of grad school. I had my PhD and no idea what I wanted to do with it."

Once Tanya let go of her hand, Miranda focused on beveling the edge of the next piece of gingerbread with a nutmeg rasp to insure a perfect fit.

Tanya was watching her intently.

"What."

"You're repurposing a tool for something other than its designed intent. That's great."

"I tried a series of files: fingernail, metal, and wood. None of them provided the correct mix of lightweight for control yet properly coarse for grinding a cookie edge. This seemed a reasonable compromise, and it worked."

Tanya simply nodded but she was still smiling like she wanted to give Miranda a gold star. Like she was twelve. Except she wasn't twelve anymore. Still not comfortable.

"How did you meet Mom and Dad?"

"There used to be an Annual Corn Roast and Fly-in at Harvey Field. A small airport just—"

"Sixty-eight-point-nine miles from here at a heading of one-two-seven to the southeast."

"Yes. Right," Tanya nodded as if of course she knew that.

Or maybe, she knew that of course *Miranda* knew that. Why wouldn't she? It was a simple fact. She could remember the first day she truly understood how FAA flight charts worked. She'd spent an entire afternoon cataloging every airport's distance and bearing from Spieden Island. How odd it must be to *not* remember something so simple and logical.

"I had only recently obtained my pilot's license and flew in along with hundreds of others for the event. Somehow I met your father there. I mentioned I had a degree and training in autism therapy, and he...sort of... brought me home. Here. To Spieden Island. Your mom was skeptical, but the moment I met you, I knew I had to stay. You were four and could still barely talk. You seemed to exist in one, single, stretched-out panic attack. Little did I know what you'd end up doing to my life."

"What was that?"

Tanya reached out and took one of her hands before she could pick up the next gingerbread piece to test its fit. "Look at me, Miranda."

She did as well as she could. Even with Tante Daniels it was always difficult. With *Tanya?* Much harder. But she tried.

"*You* made me who I am. And I *love* who I am."

Miranda finally did look at her, but she saw no tease, no game. Not even any Holly-like mischief, though Miranda was unsure what that might actually look like on a person's face.

"I didn't just buy that pretty little plane for the fun of it. Or because your parents paid me professional hourly rates while I lived here for most of two decades with no real expenses. I invested well, and now run a series of autism clinics all over the west coast. I focused on small towns, where children on the spectrum can be most easily lost by the system. That jet gets me to all of those obscure spots so that I can help the most kids possible."

"Oh. That sounds…nice." It was well beyond the *nice* of making cookie boxes. It was the kind of *nice* that… The English language seriously needed an overhaul.

"It is."

Miranda studied the next shape but couldn't seem to focus her eyes on it. She finally hung her head, letting her hair slide forward. "I'm sorry."

"Sorry? For what?"

"For being such a failure. All that work you did, and I'm not at all normal. I'm a crash investigator with a crashed brain. *That* is one of the few metaphors I actually can understand."

"Miranda, if I could make a neurotypical version of you," she picked up the nutmeg rasp and waved it over Miranda's head like a fairy godmother's wand, "it would be a crime. You wouldn't be *you* at all. You are a great crash investigator. How many hundreds or thousands of lives have you saved with the problems you've uncovered over the last seventeen years? That's incredible. You're incredible. The more I work with these kids, the more I'm convinced that many ASDs have been given some kind of gift way out there ahead of the rest of us, if only I can help them find it. Don't forget that you did all the hard work; I just tried to show you the way." Another of Tanya's most common sayings.

But it *was* another example of how she'd helped Miranda become a functioning, self-reliant adult. If only she could do better, then she'd be…doing better.

"But why do I feel so royally screwed-up."

Tanya set aside her magic nutmeg rasp and laughed. "Welcome to the human race."

Miranda would have to think about that. Or see how she *felt* about that.

In the meantime, she mixed up some royal icing, and fit the next piece of gingerbread solidly into place.

By the time she thought to look up, Tante Daniels no longer sat in the shadows.

Neither did Tanya.

7

CHRISTMAS MORNING WAS ALL ABOUT HOT COCOA AND baking.

Mike made a savory Chelsea bun Christmas tree laced with slivers of last night's roast beef and seasoned with gravy.

Tanya had made a loaf of the Dresden Stollen sweet bread that she made every Christmas. The years she didn't visit, Miranda would find a loaf in her post office box. She should have known that Tanya would be coming; there'd been no loaf waiting at the post office in town.

Her own contribution had been a big platter of eggs, bacon, and maple sausage.

And of course there were cookies. They'd packed each box tightly with her favorites. Miranda had insisted that they needed to pack all four, even though Tanya had arrived. She could take it away with her.

There weren't just sugar cookies and coconut macaroons, but also giant Paul Bunyan everything cookies, ginger-cubed shortbread with a dark chocolate ganache, peanut butter breakfast bars topped with shredded coconut, and Italian panforte. There were still plenty of leftovers.

Rather than eating at the table, they treated that as the buffet, then gathered at the other end of the great room.

The towering bay window looked out on the broken sunlight lancing through gaps in the retreating clouds. The curve of the island rolled down to the water, still wind-whipped into foaming spray where it ran between the conifer-covered islands that dotted Puget Sound.

Knowing everyone was coming, she'd cut down a big tree this year, an eight-footer that was covered with lights and years' of kid ornaments. Many had been made by her with Tanya's help. Once she'd started making them, it was hard to stop so there were dozens upon dozens of them in every size and shape she'd been able to imagine.

Much to her surprise, there were also gifts under the tree.

"Hey, I said no gifts."

"So, we broke the rules. Or Mike and Jeremy did. You know that I always do everything you say, Miranda."

Since she knew quite the opposite was true of Holly, Miranda suspected that it was all Holly's doing.

As she'd broken her own rules, it was hard to complain too much.

First there were a number of gag gifts. The funnest one was a party pack of wooden planes little bigger than her hand. Slip the wing through the slot in the fuselage, stick the little tail piece in another slot in the back, and throw.

Soon there were planes in dozens of styles and paint jobs scattered up and down the length of the great room.

She and Tanya exchanged the first real gifts.

The hand-knit cashmere scarf she'd found of the San Juan Islands seemed to make Tanya very happy.

"It's representative though not an accurate depiction of the San Juans," she explained. "It has trees made of knits and purls, waves in chaotic patches, and a cable down the middle that looks like a boat wake."

Tanya put it on immediately and declined to take it off even though they were inside. At Miranda's offer to turn up the heat, Tanya shooed her back into her chair.

Her own gift was a luxurious terrycloth bathrobe. She pulled it on, not because she was cold be because it was so cozy. Now she understood why Tanya didn't need the heat turned up but still wore her scarf.

She'd spent a long time hunting for just the right gift for the others.

Mike opened his first.

"It's the Benchmade Table Knife. Holly said they were known for making really good fighting knives. They only make the one chef's knife, but I added the black-anodized tactical grade steel. It should stay sharp for much longer than most knives."

When he finally spoke, it was so softly that she could barely hear him. "I'm going to have to cook dinner all over again now that I have the proper knife to do it. Thank you, Miranda."

Holly inspected it carefully before turning to

Miranda. "Damn fine blade, Miranda. Well done, you." Then she winked, which Miranda would take to mean that Holly had, for once, actually meant what she'd said.

Jeremy had always carried the largest pack for his site investigation tools, but it was just an open-top camper's bag. If he wanted a tool from the bottom, he had to empty the whole bag. She'd had a custom bag designed with numerous pockets and pouches of varying sizes, all separately accessible. Once he had unzipped, rezipped, and unzipped again each pocket several times, and stopped saying how perfect it was, he rushed up to his room, brought the old bag down, and was soon happily tucking tools and instruments in one pocket then another to find the best arrangement.

Holly had been tough, until she remembered the hats that she always made the team wear. They were bright yellow, billed caps for her favorite soccer team, the Australian Matildas all-women champions.

"Season tickets to...Who are the Thorns?"

"They're not the Matildas, but they're one of the better all-women soccer teams in the US. They play just a few hours south of your Gig Harbor team house in Portland, Oregon. I purchased seats for all four of us for the season. So, whenever we aren't out on an investigation we can—"

Holly screamed, leapt over the coffee table, barely missed flattening Tanya, and clamped Miranda into a crushing embrace.

"—all go together," Miranda barely managed to complete her sentence properly for lack of air.

Holly actually had tears in her eyes as she nearly

throttled Miranda again before collapsing onto the couch beside her.

"Well, Miranda, you've certainly made the rest of us look like total slackers." She draped an arm over Miranda's shoulders and kept her in a hard hug.

There was only one tiny present left under the tree.

Mike fetched it very solemnly and handed it to her.

Miranda reminded herself to look pleased no matter what it was. Something Tante Daniels had taught her, back when she was still Tante Daniels.

She carefully undid the paper.

Holly just growled beside her, "Of course you're one of *those* people."

"What people?"

"Ones who unwrap rather than tear and shred."

Miranda looked down at the box and considered. Unwrapping...*felt* right.

"I am," and she continued until she had the jewelry-sized box exposed. She opened the blue velvet case. There was a note inside that simply said, *Look behind you.*

So she turned and did.

Her quilt from the upstairs library was draped over something hanging on the wall.

Miranda circled the couch, rather than leaping over it as Holly had, and gently removed the quilt. Somehow, without her noticing while she was sculpting, a glass display case had been mounted there. Inside were planes.

Some were diecast models the size of her palm.

Others were elegant crystal little bigger than her thumb.

A few were plastic toys.

But they were all very distinct and easily identifiable for their model type. And there were so many.

"We had Jeremy go through his log of all your reports. This is every plane you've ever investigated. It took some hunting, but we think we've got them all."

Miranda could only stare at them in surprise. The monstrous C-5 Galaxy, her second crash investigation, was barely two inches long. It was dominated by an A-10 Thunderbolt II, a far smaller craft in real life. Boeing's 757 was there, along with an Airbus 320 passenger jet that sat beside a two-passenger Cessna 152 whose model was exactly the same size.

And in the center, at a place of honor, was a four-inch metal diecast F-86 Sabrejet.

Jeremy came up beside her. "You didn't actually investigate a crash on that one, but you did make an emergency landing on the National Mall, so I think that counts."

"Every one of those," Mike waved a hand at the cabinet, "represent a crash solved, recommendations for future safety made, people taken care of."

"It's—" Miranda hated unfinished sentences, but despite several attempts, couldn't find the end to this one. Tanya was right. Miranda *had* done something pretty amazing with her "crashed" brain.

"I think she likes it a wee bit," Holly was chuckling.

"It too bad my gingerbread model won't fit in this case."

"What do you mean?"

Miranda led her and the others over to the kitchen

counter. She lifted up the tea towel that was covering her finished gingerbread sculpture.

Her original plan had been to build a gingerbread F-86 Sabrejet, which had made her say what she'd just said. But that was before she'd recalled making the last-minute change.

Once again, her...*weird* brain—that was better than crashed, wasn't it—had thrown the wrong image up in the middle of Christmas morning.

Rather than *her* jet, she'd built a to-scale model of *their* private office at the Tacoma Narrows Airport. Complete right down to Holly's couch, Jeremy's workbench, and Mike's espresso machine. It was where this team all came together.

Then she noticed that something else was there that hadn't been there when she'd finished just before dawn.

There were people.

Four little people.

That's what Jeremy must have been working on yesterday.

A gingerbread Mike sat in his armchair looking smooth and casual. A blonde-haired Holly slouched on the couch with her gingerbread feet in mismatched socks resting on the coffee table. Jeremy sat at his workbench, and a tiny Miranda sat at her rolltop desk.

Then she looked more closely.

They were all smiling.

As everyone crowded around to point out one detail or another, Miranda put a hand to her heart. She knew, she simply knew, with no doubts, that this is what Christmas was supposed to feel like.

RAIDER (EXCERPT)

IF YOU ENJOYED THAT, BE SURE YOU
DON'T MISS MIRANDA NEXT
ADVENTURE.

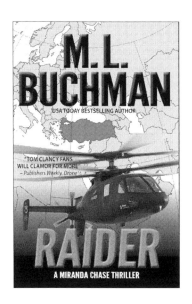

RAIDER (EXCERPT)

Ankara, Turkey
Siberkume – Cyber Security Cluster
Subbasement #2

METIN STRUGGLED AGAINST THE COLLAPSING CODE RACING
up his computer screen.

The American satellite's onboard software was self-correcting—constantly checking its synchronization and alignment.

His right-hand computer screen showed the geographic shift he'd managed to induce in seven of the thirty-three satellites in this single system. It wasn't systemic but, exactly as required, it was very localized.

On his central screen, the American code he had decrypted was about to rotate. Every hour, the encryption routine scrambled itself. He'd had one hour to decrypt and infiltrate his own code before the door closed again, and he'd have had to start over from scratch.

It had taken fifty-seven minutes for his program on the left screen to crack that code. That had left him only a three-minute window to alter the data broadcast that the satellites beamed downward.

After three months of trying, his first successful hack had finally told him which path he'd needed to pursue. A week to break down and rebuild his code had taken out the element of chance that had let him crack it the first time.

It still wasn't an easy task, but he'd done it! In under the required hour and targeted the exact location called for in the new mission profile.

But, between sixty minutes and sixty minutes-and-one second, the window into the American's code imploded once more into encrypted gibberish.

Metin collapsed back into his chair, drained as if he'd been on the attack for sixty hours, not sixty minutes.

The noises around him came back slowly, the same way Gaye Su Akyol eased into her Anatolian rock videos.

Siberkume was humming tonight, though with a very different tune.

In the big room's half-light that made it easier to stay focused on the screens, there sounded the harsh rattle of keys, soft-murmured conversations, and quiet curses of code gone wrong. It washed back and forth across the twenty stations crammed into the concrete bunker like a familiar tide. The sharp snap of an opening Red Bull can sounded like a gunshot. He liked that the Americans—all it took was watching the many eSports players Red Bull sponsored to know he belonged—were running on the same fuel he was, but still he'd beaten them.

He snapped his own Red Bull because he definitely needed something to fight back the shakes from the sustained code dive.

Siberkume might not have the vast banks of hackers like the Russians or Chinese, but he was part of a lean, mean, fighting machine.

General Firat came striding up to his station like he owned the world. Since he ran Siberkume, he certainly owned Metin's world.

"I'm sorry, General. That was the best I could do this time." It was the Cyber Security Cluster's first real test of their abilities against a force like the Americans. *He* was the one who'd done it, but it was better to be cautious with the military. Their moods were more unpredictable than his sister's crazy cat.

"No, Metin. That was a very good start. Very good. You are *çacal*—'like the coyote'."

General Firat thumped him hard enough on the shoulder that his keyboarding would be ten percent below normal speed for at least an hour.

But "Metin the Coyote"?

He could get down with that. It was seriously high praise.

"I'll get the effective window wider, General. I don't know if I can beat the hourly reset. But now that I know how to get in, I can hone my code. I'll make it faster so we have more time." Though he had no idea how. He'd already streamlined it with every trick he knew to beat that one-hour limit.

Unless he could talk his way onto the Yildiz SVR supercomputer...

Wouldn't that be *hot shit?* (He loved American slang and ferreted it out whenever he could sneak online.)

"Yes, yes." Clearly the General hadn't understood a word of what he'd said about what could and couldn't be done.

Metin considered simplifying it, but he wasn't sure how. It didn't matter; General Firat didn't pause for a breath.

"Be ready. You have one week for the next level test. You are the very first one to make it through. Your skills have not gone unnoticed. Well done, *Çacal.* Bravo!" The general must mean it as he said the last loudly enough to be easily overheard by the ten closest programmers before striding off into the dim shadows of Siberkume.

Metin grinned across the aisle at Onur.

Onur groaned, but Metin didn't rub it in too much. Onur's sister Asli was the most lovely girl in the world, and his ability to visit with her, without appearing to visit with her, depended largely on Onur's continuing friendship.

But to rub it in a little, he rolled back his shoulders and pushed out his chest like Blackpink's Rosé being so nice and just a little nasty. They'd watched all of the group's K-pop videos over a totally illegal VPN to YouTube. It was one of the luxuries of working at Siberkume: access to the outside world—if you didn't get caught.

I've so got the stuff.

Onur snorted and gave him an Obi-Wan Kenobi,

Yeah, right! look. Onur didn't look anything like Ewan McGregor, even with the expression. Of course, he himself didn't look much like the superhot Rosé.

———

Get Raider. *The next Miranda Chase adventure.*
Available at fine retailers everywhere.
Raider

ABOUT THE AUTHOR

USA Today and Amazon #1 Bestseller M. L. "Matt" Buchman started writing on a flight south from Japan to ride his bicycle across the Australian Outback. Just part of a solo around-the-world trip that ultimately launched his writing career.

From the very beginning, his powerful female heroines insisted on putting character first, *then* a great adventure. He's since written over 60 action-adventure thrillers and military romantic suspense novels. And just for the fun of it: 100 short stories, and a fast-growing pile of read-by-author audiobooks.

Booklist says: "3X Top 10 of the Year." PW says: "Tom Clancy fans open to a strong female lead will clamor for more." His fans say: "I want more now...of everything." That his characters are even more insistent than his fans is a hoot.

As a 30-year project manager with a geophysics degree who has designed and built houses, flown and jumped out of planes, and solo-sailed a 50' ketch, he is awed by what is possible. More at: www.mlbuchman.com.

Other works by M. L. Buchman: *(* - also in audio)*

Other works by M. L. Buchman:

Contemporary Romance (cont)

Love Abroad
Heart of the Cotswolds: England
Path of Love: Cinque Terre, Italy

Where Dreams
Where Dreams are Born
Where Dreams Reside
Where Dreams Are of Christmas*
Where Dreams Unfold
Where Dreams Are Written

Science Fiction / Fantasy

Deities Anonymous
Cookbook from Hell: Reheated
Saviors 101

Single Titles
The Nara Reaction
Monk's Maze
the Me and Elsie Chronicles

Non-Fiction

Strategies for Success
Managing Your Inner Artist/Writer
Estate Planning for Authors*
Character Voice
Narrate and Record Your Own
Audiobook*

Short Story Series by M. L. Buchman:

Romantic Suspense

Delta Force
Th Delta Force Shooters
The Delta Force Warriors

Firehawks
The Firehawks Lookouts
The Firehawks Hotshots
The Firebirds

The Night Stalkers
The Night Stalkers 5D Stories
The Night Stalkers 5E Stories
The Night Stalkers CSAR
The Night Stalkers Wedding Stories

US Coast Guard

White House Protection Force

Contemporary Romance

Eagle Cove

Henderson's Ranch*

Where Dreams

Action-Adventure Thrillers

Dead Chef

Miranda Chase Origin Stories

Science Fiction / Fantasy

Deities Anonymous

Other
The Future Night Stalkers
Single Titles

Printed in Great Britain
by Amazon